Haw Kola

A Lakot a Fall

By S. T. Kesler

1

Muttchen barked with excitement and raced toward the far-off grove. A single crow flew up squawking with indignation.

"They're here. They're here," Emma cried, running to the door to peer out. No one else paid much attention. For the past week, they'd heard her say the same words several times a day with the same result. No one was there.

The two young settlers knew when the trees turned russet and gold and the wind brought a chill, they could expect a visit from their Lakota friends, members of the local band. Every autumn, the tribe traveled through the north forty on their annual hunt to replenish their fresh food supply. The hunt for deer or elk needed to conclude before the bitter cold and snow of a Minnesota winter set in. As friends will do, the hunting party would stop by the family's farmhouse for a night or two before entering the deep forest in search of game.

Several young Lakota came along with the party. Emma and Heinrich were lucky because a two of them were near their same age. For a pioneer youngster, any time they could spend with others their age outside of school was both rare and special. The two farm kids had met the young Lakota's when they came on their brief visits in other times of the year. Heinrich thought Chayton was the best, much more fun than the kids in the village. He showed Heinrich how to use a bow and, in return, Heinrich would take his friend to the local fishing hole. Mamma packed them a tin with thick-cut bread sandwiches and the two headed off for the day. Heinrich had learned not to share anything about their adventures because the one time he did, the other teens in the village teased him about being an Indian lover.

Fortunately, Papa and Mama always welcomed visitors, even when the tribe's visit interrupted the normal farm routine. Everyone, including Heinrich and Emma, the youngest of three in the family, worked hard and put in long hours of hard work to make the isolated farm successful. Chores filled their days. Planting and harvesting of the food crops they cultivated to feed the family, as well as alfalfa and grass planted for animal feed lasted from spring through the summer. A bad crop meant meager meals for man and beast. In pioneer life, only toddlers lacked assigned tasks. Emma 's responsibility was feeding the chickens and geese and collecting their eggs. Heinrich helped with the crops, fetched the cows each day for milking and worked with the older boys and the men during threshing time for grain came round. On more moderate winter days, the younger generation walked several miles to attend a one-room schoolhouse where they learned to read, write, cipher and study English.

Little of the worrisome news filtering in about their parents' adopted nation or the day's events in Minnesota--now a state for over two years--reached them. Books were scarce and expensive, and Papa seldom picked up a copy of the town's weekly newspaper when he went to town for provisions. The last few visit though, Heinrich sensed he seemed more worried when he returned. Later, at night, he would overhear Mama and Papa talking in serious tones. Once he overheard his father saying, "I thought I'd escaped such nonsense when we came to the new world."

3

Sunday was a family day and a day of rest following the morning's church service. After their midday dinner, they read, played board games, and popped popcorn. Mid-afternoon on an October Sunday, a loud racket erupted in the yard, interrupting the day such with such a din of honking and wing flapping resonating from the flock of what Papa called their guard birds. A goose racket outside could mean only one thing, Emma thought, *Mika and Chayton must be here*. She ran to her brother, exclaiming, "They're here. They're here!! This has to be a hunting party from the Lakota village. I hope our friends came along. Come, Heinrich, let's go to the gate and welcome them."

Heinrich glanced over at Mama and Papa, who nodded with a smile. "We'll be joining you soon."

The two raced to the gate with big grins, but no shoes or sweaters. They didn't need to wear them until after a killing frost—which had arrived late this year.

"*Hua*. Hello," they said looking for their friends among the buckskin-clad men. The two had learned a few Lakota words along with their native tongue. Spotting Mika, Emma squealed with excitement. The two Lakota youngsters were walking alongside their fathers. The hunters stopped short a distance away waiting for Papa, too quiet, not talking or laughing. Heinrich noticed two of the young warriors limped and another had his arm in a sling.

"What's the matter with them? Emma asked. "Aren't they glad to see us? They usually are."

"Don't be silly, Emma," he answered in a know-it-all big brother tone.

Seconds later Papa emerged through the gate and trudged down the path to great the newcomers.

Wamdisapa, chief of the band and leader of this hunting party, nodded and waved to a young man carrying a large fresh-caught fish. "For you, my friend."

"Mama, come," the farmer called. "Come look at what they have brought and bring the pot of soup to share. Heinrich, help your mother," he ordered.

Piping hot from the wood stove, Mama shoveled huge spoonfuls into whatever would hold the stew like soup—serving the elders first, then other adults, and any that remained to the children. They ate and said the customary and expected things offered at such an event.

After all, had finished the meal, Papa told the youngsters they could go play. Heinrich and Chayton strolled down the lane. With them well out of earshot, he turned to ask the chief, "I see some of your braves are injured. The settlers, again? Would you need fresh cloth for bandages?"

To ask earlier would have been a grave breach of Lakota etiquette. The bad blood between the nearby settlement and the Lakota whose land they occupied once again evidenced in bloodshed.

Two

The Lakota leader laughed and tipped his head in the direction of the two young men. "Not this time, my friend. The hurt was self-inflicted. The *mazawakan* fascinate our young warriors. Every year when we ready for the hunt, someone gets hurt. Life was simpler when we followed the old ways and did not use the white man's weapons."

"*Ach, ja,*" the other replied. "Gun loading takes practice.'

After the initial exchange, the two men picked up the ritual stone pipe, which they handed back and forth. Emil learned early smoking the sacred herb, tobacco, was a gesture of peace and their friendship for the Lakota. The two conversed in a mixture of their native languages. Ten years before, Emil, his wife Hilda, and baby Herman had emigrated from Europe to this part of the north woods of the Minnesota territory, now a state. They were unique because they accepted the Lakota villagers as neighbors and legitimate inhabitants in the area. Other settlers did not. Emil's neighbors might not understand nor choose to learn a "savage tongue," but as the long friendship grew between the two men, they both endeavored to learn enough of the other's language to make themselves understood.

Emil held up his right hand and wiggled his three fingers. "Guns maim and kill—farm machinery as well. I am fortunate not to succumb to a bullet in my military days and that neither of my sons has suffered an injury since we took up farming."

Once again, the two men, one dark and clad in buckskin, the other light with a bushy beard, fell into a polite silence until Emil shot a questioning glance and spoke, "You are very early this time for the autumn hunt. How will you track the deer when there is no snow to guide you?"

"I had little choice but to lead the men of the village into the forest. Everyone is hungry. The Great Chief of the white men has not sent the food or other provisions promised to all the Lakota bands if they allowed white men, like you, to move onto and live on our ancestral lands. The elders have left on the long journey hoping to meet with him, but we cannot wait until they return. My people are hungry. Like you, I must feed my family."

Emil shook his head in disgust. "We came to the new world lured by the promise of land. I did not know the land offered was a slice of your ancestral land. A promise made should be a promise kept. If this government is untrustworthy, our future bodes ill. My friend, I am only one man, but, if you or your village are hungry or in need—ask and I will do what I can."

"No one has done more. The free access you've given us across the land you tend and the hospitality you've shown says this is so. You labor mightily on this land to provide food for your family. If the rains are few or the winter too harsh and too long, you, too, feel the gnawing of hunger. When food is plentiful, even a proud man accepts what you offer. If not, no Lakota would steal from a friend."

"And you honor your traditions by sharing what you brought down on the hunt. My children have eaten well from your bounty."

The Lakota bent his head but said nothing. The silence between the two men weighed heavy between them.

"I apologize for my fellow settlers," Emil said. "They shame themselves when they do not share with their neighbors, white or red. Where I come from, with famine also comes war."

"Already I hear rumors of such. Let us hope our elders are successful." Wamdisapa sighed and added, "Some young hotheads in the band strut about and boast of their prowess. They speak of war to take what the Lakota is due."

The two nodded and fell silent once more.

"You white men seem to hold war in higher regard than the Lakota. In our tradition, we see war always as a last resort. The old ways require respect for other persons and their property, and yes, sharing one's earned goods and food with those in need. We see bravery as a freely given offering of one's life in battle so the village can survive."

Emil grew sad. He remembered his years as a conscript in the King's army in his former homeland where war and warlike ways made up the fabric of society. Martial music dominated every parade.

"I had hoped to leave that all behind me... my brother perished on the battlefield. The glory of war died for me that day."

Wamdisapa answered in the elegant manner and the formal speech typical of the Lakota. "His souls live on—one to roam the spirit world, one to join with nature and the others to live on in the body of a baby born when your brother's souls go free to seek another body. Perhaps one followed you across the water and lives in a child near here. Perhaps in one of your children."

Emil's perplexed feelings did not find voice as he considered how much his eldest son resembled his dead brother. The thought was comforting, but short- lived as the laughter and screams of the young voices burst the reflective mood of the two men.

"Papa, Papa, we saw a bear, big with brown fur. We really did. Chayton called it a mathoe. Don't you think that a funny word? Heinrich said we needed to leave right away because her babies might be close by and she'd be mad. Isn't that exciting?"

Wamdisapa shot his son an annoyed glance. "Did you not see the *mato honkcha*?"

"Chayton, Chalon, what does matohonkcha mean?" piped Emma.

Chayton hesitated, deciding how to describe bear dropping and felt relief when Emil asked the same question.

Hearing the question in her native language, Emma put her hand to her mouth and said, "Eew!"

Mika wrinkled her nose and echoed Emma's thought, "*Seechahmeenee!*"

Both men said in their own language, "Listen well, you must stay alert in the forest. Dangers, big and small, lurk all about, hidden in the thickets. The bear was only one of many dangerous animals who might have harmed you."

Three

I think we must leave now, my friend," the Lakota said, gathering up his belongings and giving the signal to members of his hunting party. "Dusk comes soon. We must show our host our appreciation and bundle up what they have shared with us."

The young men took care pouring the remainder of the stew into pottery containers and emptying the salt and pepper shakers. If they abandoned any of the shared meal, they shamed their hosts. Leaving any food sent a message saying the meal was not generous enough or good enough—a harsh indictment.

"How long will you hunt?" Emil asked.

"Until the snow gets too deep for us to move at will while we track the game. The snow masks our scent, and footprints in the snow provide a good map, but in time the cold chills our souls."

Emil nodded. "Good hunting, my friend, be safe," he said standing up.

The Wartenburg family stood, shoulders touching, and watched the Lakota band disappear into the forest. Emil was well aware the hunters faced risks from both the forest dangers and the majority of white settlers in the area they crossed. Welcoming family farms like his were rare in northwestern Minnesota. Swatting one of the ubiquitous mosquitos yet another time, Emil said, "Na ja, Kinder. Take advantage of how near the trees are and gather up some fallen branches to use as kindling in the stoves this winter."

They scurried to their task, and their parents returned to the farmhouse.

That night with the kids down for the night, Emil and Hilda sat together near the pot-bellied wood stove in the front room. Both cradled a cup of tea on their knee and munched on a slice of almond kuchen. The children slept upstairs out of earshot of adult conversation. The bed they slept on was a rope bed with a straw mattress covered with heavy comforters.

Emil wiped the sugar from his mouth and said, "I am worried about our Lakotas and about our family, as well. What I read and hear in Taylorsville reminds me too much of the wars in the old country. I talked with Pastor Schmidt on my last visit to town and he passed on the news he gets through the church network, more reliable than what appears in the newspaper. The southern states have declared their independence and set up another country they call the Confederate States. The difference between the north and the south is how each section treats slavery. Here in Minnesota, slavery is illegal."

"If that is true, Emil, I'm sure all that is so far away, then why should we worry? That is their war, not ours."

"I hope you are right, Hilda, but in my experience, once war infects a nation, the sickness spreads like the plague. My years in the Imperial army, if nothing else, taught me that. I left my country and my military uniform to escape conflicts. Men die for no more reason than the self-importance and arrogance of a royal."

Hilda nodded, remembering Emil's sadness at the death of his brother. She patted her husband on the shoulder. "So wenn Gott will, we now live free.

The land is harsh and we endure hard labor with the farm work, but we answer to no prince."

Emil scratched at the scar on his thigh. Rubbing the spot was a constant unconscious habit since the enemy-of-the-moment wounded him in battle. They ran a sharp sword through the leg, narrowly missing his bone. Emil was the lucky one that day—more than half of his squad lost their lives. As their officer, he felt responsible. More so, when the next year, the enemy had become an ally.

"If this country goes to war, I don't think I will be able to don a uniform again. War no longer holds any glory for me."

"Na ja, Emil. Death and dying, no matter how just the cause, is still death and dying."

He squeezed her hand. Both lapsed into silent contemplation. Emil remembering the brother he lost and Hilda reliving her worry when their Duke, and later, the Kaiser himself sent her husband into war. No matter how many letters she received, no matter how many encouraging comments, until she saw him again alive and unhurt, she would worry.

"I hear Mr. Lincoln is a good man who does not want war," she said.

"So, they say, but no amount of good intentions can stop men determined to take up arms in defense of their lives and property. Men in the so-called Confederate states consider a black slave property, the same as a horse or cow. The people in the northern states consider a slave a person, albeit one of an inferior nature. Not so different from the way most view our Lakota friends."

"But that's wrong, Emil. The pastor says all are God's children and made in His image," Hilda objected.

"Well and good, Mama, the fly in the soup is what makes a man. Never underestimate the power of hate and disdain."

"Well, then, let us hope the war stays away, closer to where Mr. Lincoln reigns. And now, Liebling, to bed with us."

Four

The next few weeks seemed to pass in a flash. The trees in the grove surrounding the farmhouse framed the building in brilliant orange, russet, and crimson. The deep red, three-leafed vines crawled up the trunks and covered the ground. Pioneer kids welcomed the color, not for the beauty, but because the bright red color and fuzzy stalks let them identify at a glance the poison ivy. The strong naphtha soap Mutti used to clean the sap off their itchy arms and ankles sometimes seemed as nasty as the plant.

With the beauty came the cold. The first hard freeze caused the plants in the garden to droop and then die. Frost iced the windows and walls every morning. The house provided shelter from the wind, but the cold penetrated the uninsulated walls. When the time to take out the eider-down comforters and hand-made quilts from storage in the attic arrived, the sleeping loft was already freezing. The cozy quilts kept the cold at bay during the night.

When the first faint rays of the sun appeared, Heinrich got up and broke the ice on the water in the washbasin. The rest of the household began to stir as Papa and Herman put on their heavy coats and gloves and headed for the barn to being the milking. Heinrich braced against the stiff wind as he made his way up the hill to the pasture to round up any stray cows not returning to the barnyard on their own. He dodged the huge brown piles of cow dropping steaming in the frigid air. Back at the farmhouse, Herman had begun his day throwing wood, and coal if there was any, into the living room stove to heat the room. Papa had banked the fire the night before. Emma's job was to put small twigs and branches into the kitchen stove and put the teakettle on one of the cast iron stovetops. Every pioneer child had a job and wore heavy clothes outside or in the chilly house in the winter

Mutti was busy, as she knew when the men returned with a hearty appetite. She placed thick slices of homemade rye bread on the table alongside a bowl of hardboiled eggs. "We need butter, Herman, and more eggs, Emma," she said.

Without argument, he put on his heavy coat and went out to the pump house for a bucket to use to bring up butter from the well. His next stop was the hen house where he threw feed outside to lure the chickens away from their nest. With most of the hens gone, he reached under each still sitting hen and extracted whatever eggs might be under her, He checked the empty nests and gathered any eggs laid there. He put his take in the bucket alongside the butter and trotted back to the house thinking, *I'll be glad when Emma is old enough to fetch feed and collect the eggs. Those nasty hens have long sharp beaks.*

The kitchen smelled wonderful to the boys when they came back inside. Aromas from the thick rashers of bacon frying in the heavy cast iron pan filled the air. Farm families ate hearty. Mama put most of the eggs he'd gathered into the water reservoir at the back of the huge wood stove to cook hard for tomorrow's breakfast. Half a dozen she kept back and set out on the back porch to use for baking later.

"Emma, lead the prayer," Papa said.

She recited as fast as she could the words she'd memorized about blessing the food and everyone and then finished with a quick, "Amen."

The knives and forks clinked and scraped against the chipped everyday dishes. Eating was serious business, making mealtime one where children were expected to be seen but not heard. Papa's chair scraped across the roughhewn wood floor. "Time for you to leave for school," he said, pointing to the tin lunch pails ready for them. This was Heinrich's last year at the one-room schoolhouse located on a small plot of land Emil and his neighbor had donated. Next year, once the snow grew too deep, he would need to join Herman and take the buckboard into town and share the room their parents rented in a boarding house. But, for now, the siblings faced only a mile-long walk to reach the building. Heinrich, as one of the three in the top class, would bring in wood to place on top of the heaped ashes covering the banked embers of yesterday's fire—except Monday when they'd find the room freezing cold, a signal they needed to rebuild the fire completely.

The students filed in, saying "Good morning, Miss Koepp," before they took their seats. Little kids like Emma sat in front in the small desks, the oldest in big desks in the back. As Heinrich sat down, the boy behind him snickered and whispered, "I saw your pet savages visited you again. Ain't you got better ways to use your time."

With a wham, bam, bam of her ruler, Miss Koepp brought the chatter to an end.

Five

Heinrich clenched his hands into fists and clenched his jaw. Adolf deserved a quick punch in the jaw for making nasty remarks about folks he didn't even know. With an effort, he let out a breath he didn't realize he'd been holding and relaxed his fists. Save it for later, he thought. He had no inclination to become better acquainted with Miss Koepp's wicked backhand. Did that once, and once was enough.

When the little kids in front were reciting or reading aloud, Adolf, one row behind Heinrich delivered a barrage of jeers about painted savages, ignorant insect eaters, murderous killers, shifty sticky-handed thieves. Heinrich tried to tune him out without success. "Later, *Arschloch*," he hissed at the troublemaker behind him. Adolf was a year older, taller, and heavier than Heinrich, albeit dumber, but by the end of the day, his frustration with Adolf exceeded his normal good sense. Heinrich listened to Miss Koepp with half an ear and stared at his textbook not reading a word as he planned to confront the enemy.

When the bell rang for the end of school, everyone put away their books, covered the ink in the inkwell on their desks, and retrieved the tin lunch pails they'd brought with them. Heinrich caught Helga, a neighbor kid, attention and waved her over, "I've got some business to take care of after school. Can you take Emma with you?"

Helga gave his younger brother an odd look. "Is this about that dreck-loser Schmidt's nonsense? If you're smart, you'll just consider the source and ignore him. He's not worth wasting any of your time or effort over."

"Na ja, if what he was saying was about me, I'd just tell him to eat crap, but he's talking about Chayton and the rest of the Lakota. That's not right."

"Your funeral, my friend," Helga said with a shrug.

Heinrich entered the schoolyard and spotted Adolf at the far end, surrounded by his gang of bullies. *Not taking you on, here, you idiot. You're on foot and I know the way you go home.*

As a diversion, he started down the path toward his own farm, which lay in the opposite direction from Adolf's. Once out of sight of the gang in the schoolyard, Heinrich circled back around through the trees in the grove of the school's neighbor. He slid his book bag off, placing the denim sack in a knothole in a nearby giant oak. He wrapped his handkerchief around one hand, the scarf around the other the way he'd seen a boxing match at a fair once and the cloth might work as a substitute for gloves.

The wait was not long. Adolf was alone as he was the only one who lived up this road. Heinrich waited until the other boy was nearly on him before leaping out and demanding, "Ready to take back what you said about our friends, schtinkszeifer?"

"In your dreams, Lakota-lover. You're welcome to all the smelly savages you want. My friends and I prefer our friends white and smart enough to know how to read and write," Adolf said, as he stepped forward and threw the first punch.

Heinrich expected this and stepped to one side, throwing a punch in the other direction the way he'd seen boxers do. This punch landed, the next five did not. Meanwhile, Adolf got his licks in with two – landing one to the midsection, the other to the jaw. Soon both boys were rolling around on the ground, pummeling each other. The fight abruptly ended when Adolf grabbed Heinrich's arm and bit down hard. Startled, Heinrich slammed the side of his hand down on the larger boy's neck, causing him to curl up and gasp for breath. Heinrich's reflexes came into play and brought his knee up between the older boy's legs.

"Cat got your tongue? That'll teach you to bite me. Maybe you've learned a little respect for me and my friends."

Adolf gasped for breath and held his groin. Red-faced, he growled something unintelligible and spun, making his way down the path. Heinrich turned and scurried off in the opposite direction toward home. Neither boy noticed Miss Koepp taking in the whole thing with a grim look on her face. She stood tossing her swat stick from hand to hand.

As he entered the barnyard, Emma spotted him. "Are you ever going to be in trouble now," she squealed. "You're all dirty and your shirt torn. Papa and Mama will be so mad at you."

"Quiet, pipsqueak."

In his heart, Heinrich knew she was right. Convinced more so when his father came up behind the two and said in a stern voice, "Fetch a switch, young man. Your behavior is not acceptable. Spare the rod, spoil the child, my father always used to say. We do not tolerate street brawlers in this house."

He handed Heinrich his knife and waved toward the grove and began one of the longest walks of his young life. Reaching the overgrown ground beneath the towering trees, he carefully cut a switch a little wider than two fingers. Looking first both ways to see if anyone were watching, he moved on and sliced off a much thinner stick resembling a willow branch. I'll try this one first. Maybe I'll get lucky.

He hid the thicker branch behind a blackberry bramble and walked across the farmyard to his father. Crossing his fingers, he handed over the slender excuse for a switch. His father took the rod from him, lifting and swinging the implement. Heinrich could swear he saw the hint of a smile creeping up the corners of his father's mouth.

"I think not, son. If you were half the age of Emma, perhaps, but you are well beyond that. Get a more useful switch at once—or would you rather I got out my razor strop and saved you a trip?"

Heinrich made haste to shake his head back and forth hard. "No, sir," he said, hitching up his trousers and heading back to the grove where he'd hidden the alternate switch. He carried the birch wood implement to his father without a word.

"Drop your drawers and bend over," Emil commanded.

Heinrich swallowed hard and followed orders.

Emil put his hand up, licking his finger to see which direction the wind was coming from, shook the switch up and down and made a circular motion. He moved his hand up the stalk a bit and swung backward with force. And stopped. "Hmph, wrong angle," he said and stepped to the left half a step.

Another wind-up, a swift descent, a sudden hesitation and impact. As always, the threat was worse than the event, more so because the recipient never knew if the next time the blow might be full force. Heinrich braced himself several times before the switch landed with authority at last.

"Let that teach you to leave brawling to the Swedes."

"Ja, ja, Papa."

They both knew the switch and the swings were more for show than any real hurt. Most of Heinrich's friends were not so lucky. Their fathers always used a sturdy switch or, worse, their belt or razor strop—and wielded them with more enthusiasm and more often.

Father and son smiled the smile of a shared secret. Some things Mama did not need to know.

But Heinrich knew next time he might not be as lucky.

Six

Early the next morning, a raucous racket rose from the grove—the pete-pete-pete sound of pheasants disturbed by an intruder—wakened the household. The noise was not quite the ruckus grouse might make, the repetitive cries sufficed to wake a light sleeper like Heinrich or his father. Although Heinrich shared his tendency to sleep light, Emil attributed his hair-trigger wakefulness as a survival skill learned listening for the enemy on the battlefield.

The boy hopped up, paused by the chamber pot, broke open the ice formed over the water in the wash basin, pulled on a shirt and trousers over his long underwear, and headed downstairs. He threw open the door on the stove and stirred the ashes before heading outside for wood—and to check out what upset the birds. Maybe a fox or even a wolf too close to the house might be a possum riled them up. I'll need to go out into the grove and see.

Heinrich's buttocks still bore witness to their unfortunate experience of the day before. He scratched at one and pulled his trousers from between. Much better than a night with no dinner.

Not once did he consider what he'd do if the intruder turned out to be a wolf or a bear. He put one hand over his eyes to shield them from the sun and stared intently. One flock flew up and, after an interval, another, and then another. Heinrich had learned from his friend Chayton; the Lakota viewed this pattern as an announcement member of the tribe or other guests were about to arrive.

A squirrel up a tree started a racket, scolding his displeasure at being disturbed. A possum waddled out of the brush hissing. Several crows and one blue jay added to the din. Whatever was out there was imposing enough to catch the attention of nearly every creature. Heinrich did not see or hear anything revealing the intruder.

Then a sharp "snap, crack" sounded behind him. His mind filled with images of animals with teeth, he jumped and whirled to face the intruder.

"What are you doing out here?" Emma asked.

"'The question, little sister, is what are you doing out here by yourself?' Didn't Papa tell you to always come out here with Herman or me? —Not that any self-respecting wolf pack would consider you much of a meal."

She pushed forward with an aim of sharing a reminder punch in his midsection but fell flat on her face instead. She twisted around pulling at her skirt, which had caught on a bramble bush. Heinrich hurried to help her. She scarcely had freed herself when the underbrush nearby moved followed by, "Hau, Heinrich. Hau, Emma."

Chayton emerged from the thicket, trailed by Mika. Big smiles all around as the four unlikely friends exchanged gestures of greeting.

The two girls paired off, talking at each other so fast neither understood the other. The two boys stood back watching. "Girls can act so silly."

"Emma, take Mika and run back to the farmhouse. Let the rest of the family know our friends are back from the hunt." He glanced over at Chayton and added, "We'll wait for you here."

"My father sent us ahead to let you know they were coming. They wanted to finish butchering the deer and gather berries and mushrooms before they came. They need to cut most of the meat into strips for drying."

The girls scurried off to alert the family, and the boys sat on a convenient log a few feet away. "'Tell me all about it, Chayton. I so wish I could go with you sometime. Mama says my going along can't happen--it's simply isn't done. Whatever that is supposed to mean. "

"I don't think I've ever seen wasichu on a hunting party. Don't any of your people ever hunt? I think we'd be a great team."

"I wish I could go with you sometime, but Papa says the reason we don't go hunting is because we raise animals on the farm, but that's no fun. Some of our neighbors do – head out into the fields with shotguns for birds. Not us. Papa's thinking slaving with pigs and chickens is better. I say they are nothing but hard work. You've don't know how lucky you are, living as you do. Free and all."

"Butchering is hard work, too. The women do most of the work. When we have a good hunt, we eat well. Otherwise…" Chayton's voice trailed off. "Maybe pigs and chickens aren't all bad."

"Papa keeps preaching about how important storing our crops can be. We have a special building to store some of last year's crop, just in case," Heinrich said. Our father keeps talking about the late planting and how small the crops are--seems pretty worried. A lot of the farmers are. I hope they're wrong."

"I've been hungry," Chalon admitted. "That's hard, so hard. Two winters ago, my baby sister didn't get enough to eat so she got sick and died. I was so sad. I was hungry and my stomach ached, but losing my sister made my heart ache more."

Seven

Emil came out of the farmhouse wiping his hands on a towel from the kitchen. Unlike most fathers in the settler community, he often volunteered to help his wife with carrying the heavy cast iron pots to begin the process. Hilda had rendered one batch of tallow from the two pigs they'd slaughtered. Cooking down the thick stinky stuff and adding the lye to make bars of soap for doing laundry and dishes was hard work. Today's job was to finish another batch of the strong soap in the giant-sized cookers. She planned a smaller batch of less strong soap as well with a fragrance added to use for bathing and face washing. She had elderberries and wildflowers gathered to provide the perfume.

The timing of the Lakota band's arrival was fortunate. Being late in the day, Emil and Hilda had the mixture already poured into a flat pan to set. Cutting the hardened soap was a task for tomorrow. Emil glanced up at the sun, saying to Wamdisapa, "Welcome, my friend. Have you eaten?"

"We come with food to share. Our hunt went well. Our bellies will be full through the winter. For now, we've enough to feed us all."

He beckoned to a tall brave to join them, and the young man produced a huge haunch of venison. Emil and Hilda made all the proper noises to say how impressed they were at the size of the hunk of meat and how fine it appeared.

"Heinrich, Herman, come. Take Chayton with you and gather up corncobs and put them under the spit. "If there aren't enough to make a hot enough fire, you can add a few thick branches. Emma, you take Mika with you to the root cellar and collect some potatoes."

"Yes, Papa."

The two men smiled as the two girls ran off giggling. "We have berries to enjoy, also. Food is sacred to us. Not only because often an animal gave its life for us, but we know, without food there is no life, and food must, therefore, be given proper respect"

"What God provides, we must use well," Emil said in a solemn tone.

Soon the two men saw slivers of smoke rising, signaling the aromas of cooking meat. The Lakota and the pioneer family worked together to prepare their feast. They put down blankets on the ground to sit upon, boiled water to make cranberry tea. Hilda pulled out wooden trenchers for the food and tin cups for the tea. At five o'clock with only about an hour to sunset, Hilda brought out candles so they'd have light later.

Soon Lakota and settlers mingled around the fire, their usual blankets or coats over their shoulders to stave off the chilly dusk air. The size of the roast meant a longer time to cook, giving the young people more time to enjoy each other's company. Some of the other younger hunters joined their circle, sharing whatever their language skills allowed. On the other side of the fire, Hilda joined the women who'd accompanied the hunting party to gather roots and berries for the winter. Emil and Wamdisapa sat close together and shared a pipe.

Glancing at the position of the sun, Emil beckoned to come over. "Son, make sure the cows and pigs are secure and fed. Have Heinrich scatter feed for the chickens and geese."

"Yes, Papa," he said, turning to signal Heinrich and head toward the barn.

"How come we always have to go get the animals? Why can't Emma take care of the poultry?"

"Would you rather work in the kitchen washing dishes?"

"Heck, no," Heinrich snorted.

"Well then, go take care of the chickens and quit your jammering."

Heinrich shot his brother a dirty look and headed toward the flock of geese. He stopped at the feed shed and filled a bucket with goose-chicken feed. The birds roamed free and foraged for bugs and bits on their own, but as the season progressed, they needed some additional provisions. As he approached the geese, the two big drakes spread their wings and hissed. He gave them plenty of space. He'd learned from experience how aggressive geese are and how prone they were to attack. Once he had the bucket and scattered the first handful, the geese realized he was a good guy with food and posed no danger. They set about gorging themselves before roosting for the night.

Chickens next, so he headed toward the hen house where the only potential problem was a banty rooster with a bad attitude and worse temper. This bird, nicknamed *Schlechtvogel*, lived up to his name and made up for his small size with bad-tempered aggressive attitude. While some of the larger roosters might disagree, Schlechtvogel clearly considered himself king of the roost.

Heinrich was wiping his hands on the back of his trousers, banging them together to get the last of the feed off when Herman joined him. "We better get back. The meat should be done by now and we wouldn't want them to eat it all before we get there."

The two boys trotted off to join the others at the "young" side of the fire, well-filled trenchers in hand. Less talk and more chewing ensued.

Meanwhile, on the adult side of the circle, the two men and Hilda finished their meal and leaned back against the large log behind them. "Will this carry your village through the winter, my friend?"

"Whether we eat well or end up on short rations depends on how well the talks the elders have with the Great White Father go. I am worried. We met another hunting party. They told us their elders had little luck. Another Lakota band, whose village lay farther toward the setting sun, a place with few trees, made the same journey with a similar result. The Great White Father did not listen and was uncompromising. He told the other bands they'd already received ample compensation."

"I would swear I read the food and other goods would be ongoing as long as the white man lived unmolested and without interference on the tribal lands," Emil said.

"I hope you are right; the lives of my people may depend on it."

They all lapsed into silence. The alternative was too dire for idle conversation. The vision of starving children the two men had seen in their youth too graphic.

In time, the two parted, Emil to join the rest of his family asleep a warm bed with a heavy quilt. Wamdisapa pulled his blanket around his shoulder and lay as close to the warmth of the fire as he could. Here and there more than one shared a blanket, gaining body heat from each other.

Eight

The sun had scarcely crept over the horizon when the Lakota left. Group good-byes finished after the meal the night before. The family spent the night in the farmhouse, the Lakota around the fire. Only Emil was awake to bid Wamdisapa a safe trip and extend the family's welcome for a return visit.

Wamdisapa inclined his head and spoke, "You do your people proud, Emil Wartenburg."

"As do you, Wamdisapa, as do you. Perhaps one day our peoples will all become Americans."

With that, the Lakota slipped into the hazy light of dawn. Emil returned to the farmhouse to roust the rest of the family. Hilda greeted him as he entered, "Another good visit, Emil. The Lakota live their lives with honor and dignity. If only our neighbors…"

"Na Ja, *Liebchen*, if only. Why can't we all get along?"

He spun and walked the few steps to the base of the stairs calling up, "Time to get up, Kinder. Today is another day. Chores don't do themselves, and you have school today."

The two boys slouched down the stairs followed by a sleepy-eyed Emma. They sat down around the table in the kitchen and devoted their attention to the steaming hot bowls of oatmeal Mama had set at their places. A thick slice of homemade bread slathered in soft cheese completed the meal. When they finished eating, all three threw on their coats and headed out to the barn, henhouse, and other work destinations until Mama rang the small bell, the signal to leave for school.

Mama had their three lunch pails ready. "Dress warm, children and bring your scarfs. The wind is picking up and smells like snow."

The three retrieved their boots from the front porch, glad for their warm socks in the cold shoes. They buttoned their coats and trudged down the dirt road for the long walk to their one-room schoolhouse, pulling their scarfs up over their faces so their throats didn't freeze. Mama was right. The wind was brutally cold and left little doubt winter was around the corner. Even with the warm wool to protect their faces, they could see their breaths in the frigid air. All three were happy to see the smoke rising from the chimney of the schoolhouse. Miss Koepp already had the fire going.

Inside, the students who'd already arrived clustered around the stove. Most of the big kids shouldered the smaller ones aside to get closer. Heinrich glowered at the others. He grabbed Emma's hand, put their lunch buckets in front of them, and made like a Roman phalanx to push the offenders into the cold. The buckets worked as well as the shields did so long ago.

"Hey, whatcha think you're doing?" one big kid demanded.

"Only showing a little sharing and some good manners," Heinrich answered. Fortunately   for him, the teacher arrived and told everyone to take their seats.

"Primary students, take out your slates for handwriting practice. Grades four through six, take out your McGuffey's – page 57. Read the section and complete the exercises. Grades 7 and 8. Today is math day. You know what to do. Review your homework and move on to the next set of problems which we will discuss."

She rapped her ruler on the big roll-top desk and turned her attention to the small children in the first two rows. "Emma, write on the blackboard the sentence for today."

Emma stood, took the piece of chalk Miss Koepp handed her, and moved to the big blackboard at the front of the classroom. Heinrich watched her from his seat in the row in front of the largest desks. He watched his sister's slow strokes as she transcribed the sentence onto the larger surface.

Come on, Sis. You only need to push the chalk over the blackboard, not try to carve the letters into the slate"

"Heinrich, don't you have something better to do than stare into space?" Miss Koepp asked. "Please stay after school. We need to talk

"Yes, Miss Koepp," he answered and picked up his book.

Heinrich was fortunate enough to sit by a window. He stared out at the bleak grey sky. The wind picked up some and seemed to whistle around the corners of the small building. Occasionally, a downdraft on the chimney caused eddies of ashes to seep through the cracks around the door in the stove.

By midday, students had completed their assignments and clustered near the stove at the back to eat their lunches. In early fall and spring, they escaped the classroom to the outside area to eat. With the storm imminent, Miss Koepp doubted her students would see much sunlight on the long walk back to the farm. Dusk was early now, earlier more still in December and January.

Not soon enough for the older students, Miss Koepp glanced up at the big clock on the back wall. They'd already been checking the time surreptitiously. Any student caught turning around to see the clock might well find themselves given a sharp rap across the knuckles.

"Three o'clock, students. Remember to take your homework with you.," she said, and then added, "The wind is picking up, and there are snowflakes drifting down. Not many yet, but mind you go straight home. You need to hurry and stay safe."

"Yes, Miss Koepp," they chorused, filing out the door their scarves flapping.

"Heinrich, we will talk Monday when the storm has passed. Your behavior with Adolf was uncalled for and not without consequences."

The pelting grainy snow hit his face as he left and ran to catch up with his brother and sister. Altogether a fitting end for a lousy day.

Nine

The trio trooped on the porch of the farmhouse, shedding their boots and coats. They banged their boots and mittens together outside the door to remove the snow and mud. All whipped the scarves from off their faces against the wall to do the same. Small chinks of ice dropped from the woolen fabric with a muted clink. The moist air of their breaths created a mist in the unheated porch.

Emma led the way into the warm kitchen. The heat felt both good and bad against near-frostbitten faces and hands. As the blood flowed to their fingers and toes, the tingling was fierce and hurt. Mama pointed to three cups of sweet hot tea on the table. They all grabbed one and downed the first swallow. A second later, each of them spat the mouthful into the saucer under the glass. The hot liquid felt like fire to their still cold tongues. "Ouch," Emma wailed. "All my insides are burnt."

"No, the tea only feels scalding," Heinrich said. "The contrast with the cold air we were breathing makes you think the drink's too hot."

"Uh uh," she said. "How would you know what my mouth feels like?"

"Hush, Child, because your mouth complains as much as you. Let the tea cool—everything will be fine," Mama chided.

Herman arrived from town, came in, and picked up his cup and set off to the cupboard on a mission. He rummaged around, opening doors and drawers searching for a cookie. Mama made the best oatmeal cookies ever. Without turning around, Mama said," If that's a cookie you're looking for, young man, then you will need to wait until after dinner. You can have an apple now—if you go down to the root cellar and fetch some for your brother and sister."

He made a face, but set his cup back down and opened the door to the dugout space under the house they called a basement grumbling as he went. The stairs leading down to the cellar were hand-cut, each riser rough and uneven. The dirt-floored space smelled musty with mold, and the low ceiling anyone close to adult height needed to duck to avoid getting his head hit. Mama kept the apples and other long- lasting remnants of the fruit from their orchard in wooden boxes in an even-lower ceilinged space. The cool air and dark kept the fruit tasting fresh and juicy for a long time. Along one wall of the cellar, row upon row of pale green glass Mason jars sat filled with Mama's canned fruit, vegetables, and meats. This larder provided meals for the winter.

Heinrich would rather she not can okra, ground cherries, or turnips. They were a disgusting imitation of food when they were fresh, and in his opinion of no value whatever once canned. Peas and beans were fine, but corn was his all-time favorite. Papa called corn "pig food" and wouldn't eat any raw, only canned and disguised with cream.

He doesn't know what he's missing--especially if we roast them over the fire. Yum.

"Heinrich, did you fall in? Your brother and sister want their apples," Mama called down from the door at the top of the cellar stairs.

He grabbed three, hesitated, and then added two more, tucked them into an improvised a bag from his shirt, then raced up the stairs to the kitchen. Mama gave him a faint smile as she took the apples and set them on the table. She

murmured "Danke," she and the two others, chose the piece of fruit they wanted.

A stamping noise from the porch interrupted the sounds of apple

crunching. The door opened and a swirl of tail-wagging white charged in,

scattering snow and ice crystals on each young person. Muttchen, who spent

most of her days as an outside dog, pranced about, excited to be indoors and

away from the frigid cold and harsh wind.

"Emil, why is that animal in here, dirtying up my house?"

"Liebchen, no need to us to leave any animal outside in this weather. No

matter how lowly, the Christian thing to do is to give shelter. The cows are in a

barn and can stand by close to warm each other. Other animals do not fare well

under their hooves. Remember, yea, the least of them …?"

"The bible was talking about people, "she objected, but in a more mollified

tone. "Let's not make this a regular thing."

"Agreed," he answered, his faint smile and up-raised eyebrow saying the

opposite. "Boys, you need to put your coats back on after you finish your tea.

We'll need more wood closer to the house and check the cistern for the water

level, too. This storm is shaping up to be a big one—the kind the Yankees call a

northerner. A real blizzard, ja."

Herman and Heinrich grimaced at each other but donned coats, boots,

scarves, and mittens. Out the door, they soon realized the wind had grown fierce,

and gained a more icy edge since they arrived home from school. They each

brought an armful, hoping this would be enough to satisfy their father. Emil peered out from the porch and called, "Three more loads each. If this storm lasts too long, we might come up short. Even if the snow stops coming down, the drifts may be so high we won't be able to move about freely. I'll be out in a minute and string the rope from the barn and the chicken house to the back door. This will allow a safe trip. We must tend to the animals — especially the cows who'll need milking."

"The good thing about snow…," Mama began.

"Nothing's good about this much snow," Emma objected.

"How wrong you are, my dear," her mother replied as she busied herself with a large bowl, eggs, honey, and cream before adding a hearty spoonful of strawberry preserves. "Snow makes it possible for us to make…"

"Ice cream," Emma squealed. "Ice cream." She ran to the porch to announce this marvelous fact to her father and brother, "Hurry up. Mama's making ice cream. Strawberry!"

Ten

The next morning, the snow and wind seemed fiercer than the previous day. The winter continued with snow and more snow, cold, cold and more cold. Should the storm be severe enough, for the silver lining for students, was the cancellation of school, often days at a time. The sleigh became the preferred— and only—method of transportation, but even this was not possible when the winds were too strong or the temperature too cold for its runners to work as they should. Papa's estimate of three more armfuls of logs each proved far below what they needed. If the snow had drifted too deep, Papa said a day at school was not worth the risk of having a horse with a broken leg.

The snow remained up to three-foot-deep until mid-March, but April lived up to its reputation, bringing heavy rains. Heinrich remembered how dry the fields were the year before. Not this year, the rain melted the piles of snow remaining and the area flooded. The water rose to the top of the nearby creek and flowed over its bank. Papa said, "Don't let me hear you complaining about having to come uphill to the house. If we didn't, the water might have come up to the house, too."

"We're close," Heinrich said. "'We're living in a sea of mud. I can almost hear Mama say, 'Wipe your feet and take off those muddy boots' in my sleep.'"

"And the barn, too," Herman added. "The mud of the trail to the pasture is knee high. They balk when I try to herd them."

"Can't say as I blame them. There's no grass out there for them," Heinrich replied.

Papa must have come up behind them and overheard their conversation. "With luck, the hay in the barn will last until there is. We may have bigger problems, though. I doubt we'll be able to use even a single bottom plow for a long time. The furrows will fill up with water, making planting impossible."

"All we can do is wait and hope. Pray the field dries enough to plow and plant. We've a short growing season around here anyway, which means every day that passes puts us at risk for little or no crop," Papa said. A fallow flooded field means hunger for the animals and for us, too, come next winter."

The two boys stared back at him with somber expressions while Emma, oblivious, played in a puddle. The trees seemed happy with all the moisture, but everything else suffered—people the worst—their clothes attracting the mud and grime everyone hauled inside.

Then the miracle they'd been praying for arrived. The temperature in May leaped to the mid-nineties. The strawberries bloomed, and the family hastened to hitch the horse behind the plow. Papa took on the tough task and manned the plow to break open the surface of the soil. Heinrich and Herman took turns plowing a deep furrow. Lagging behind, Mama and Emma began planting the seeds for rye, oats, corn, and alfalfa. Some would become flour, some animal feed.

When the acres of row crops were in, Mama directed the efforts in the garden. The herbs and chokecherries already had sprouted or pushed out leaves, but the rain had destroyed the potatoes, cabbage and Brussel sprouts she planted as winter crops. Mama replanted and hope. Peas, beans, lettuce, tomatoes came next.

Papa and Herman went into the small fruit orchard sheltered in the space between the house and the surrounding grove and pruned the apple and, cherry trees. The quince and pears were too small to need much pruning. They cut back the black raspberries and shaped the red ones. "How did we get so many fruit plants, Papa?" asked Emma.

"Some we bought from the merchant traveling with a wagon-load of plants and shrubs. He comes every year. The others we grew from cuttings taken from neighbors' trees and they took from some from ours. Some seeds we brought with us from the old country. Let's finish up now."

Not a hint of wind cooled them as they packed up their tools and headed across the creek toward the outbuildings and the house. The cool water felt good on their bare feet. Heinrich nodded, crammed his hat down, and shielded his eyes from the sun. Overhead an enormous flock of starlings soared down, joining crows pecking at the earth for worms and other insects exposed in the plowed fields.

The sound of a bell caught their attention. "Time for dinner," the boys, chorused. "I'm starving."

The shade on the front porch where Mama had spread out the dinner was welcome. "Bring a bucket of water in. Everyone is thirsty."

The smell of sauerkraut and sausage was tantalizing. Baked beans and biscuits completed the menu. "Wash up, boys," she added.

Eating consumed all their attention and the food disappeared. Mama brought out a treat —bread pudding covered in thick cream. Herman picked up a knife and carved huge squares. "That tastes good," Papa said with a smile. "The only thing better would be apple kuchen."

"No apples left in the cellar," she said. "Apple pie will have to wait until fall. The chokecherries will be ripe soon and we can have sauce. If everyone has finished eating, get your dishes to the dishpan. I have a special project for you this afternoon." She waved her hand at a pile of clothes at the end of the porch.

The three picked through the heap. "Everything here is too small even for me," Emma said.

"You must bring straw and stuff the clothes and tie the ends of the sleeves and trousers with twine. We need scarecrows in the fields. Three should do it, I think."

When they'd stuffed the form, Herman and Heinrich shoved a heavy branch through the arms. "Come on, bring the manikins and a hammer," Herman said. "We'll hang them on the posts in the middle of the fields. "

They hoisted the three scarecrows up and stepped back to admire their handiwork only to watch the birds take notice of the new perch and land.

One crow landed, dipped, and seemed to smirk at them.

"Caw."

Eleven

Morning arrived sunny and warm—a perfect Sunday--because today was the day of the church's annual bazaar and bake-goods exchange. They all looked forward to gatherings like this one, special for the adults, but more so for the children, because the gathering in town offered one of the few opportunities for them to see their town friends again before school began. Few such days remained before everyone needed to pitch in to bring in the harvest. In a few weeks, only babies would escape the hard labor of reaping and harvesting the crop. Any child, old enough to drive the wagon, hauled loads of fresh smelling grains to the storage sheds.

At the church, long tables, covered with bright red checkered cloths, swayed from the weight of the food placed on crowding the surface, brats and beer, too. After a short hymn singing and the pastor's blessing, the crowd broke into clumps of men and women strolling and chatting while their kids played ball, tag, or king of the hill. Their younger brothers and sisters played jacks or rolled hoops in the street.

The majority of the women compared and traded recipes and reported on their garden's progress while watching the tots in the trail leading from the church to the cemetery. Two of three sat on a bench in earnest conversation while the tones of the men grew more somber despite the beer and hard cider.

Emil and his neighbor Rudolf sat on a far bench. Rudolf and Emil knew each other by reputation as both had served in the King's army in the old country and had lost friends or family. "What do you hear about the conflict in our adopted country? I must admit I don't understand why brother fights brother here, where most have come for freedom and to escape the oppression of the royalty or their lackeys," Rudolf said.

"We hear so little being so fár in the wilderness and away from the battles," Emil answered. "From the little, I read in the newspapers I see or traveling peddler or others coming through our area, I think the country is in danger of splitting into two or more sections. Americans are fighting Americans. Some say they've begun conscription, just like in our home country, the rich buy their way out. If we're not careful, they'll be dragging us in. One regiment speaking our native tongue already exists in Wisconsin. I'd hoped we left such nonsense back in the old country."

"That's terrible—I had my fill of gunpowder and spilled blood long before I brought my family here. What do we do if they start something like that around here? Where can we go to escape?" Rudolf asked.

"All we can do is wait, my friend, we wait. Some men fight for freedom, and some fight to keep freedom from others. Just pray no one learns of our military experience."

"Who are they keeping from freedom? The black men? Why should we care about their freedom any more than we would about the freedom of their owner's livestock? The only difference is we eat the animals and chickens. Next thing you know, the savages around here will get grandiose ideas, expecting more than we can grant or what they deserve—nothing but thieving bastards every one, one step above our animals, they are. They got more than they deserved when the army delivered wagon loads of provisions last year. Did my heart good to hear the army won't deliver this year."

Emil stifled a gasp. He'd heard hateful things said occasionally, but Rudolf was his good friend and he didn't expect such hate coming out of his mouth. "The Bible teaches us God didn't intend for men to be judged by the color of skin, but by the purity of their soul."

"Mein Gott, Emil, you sound like one of those nambly pambly abolitionist types. They act as great do-gooders dealing with souls until something happens and a skin problem affects their own lives. Mark my words, my friend, mark my words."

Fate intervened in the person of Emma and two of her friends. "Papa, Papa, my hoop is all bent. It won't roll. Can you fix it?"

"My goodness, Emma, what a tragedy. Bring your hoop here and let me look at the damage. Did you take this somewhere you ought not to?" He smiled over her head at Rudolf. Rudolf sent an awkward smile back.

"Maybe Uncle Rudolf can help me. I understand he is skilled at fixing things."

"Aren't I though?"

Emma's friend, bounced up with the offending toy. The two men made a great show of being engrossed in the swaybacked circle and, for now, forgot their prior argument.

Not so lucky was Heinrich, who'd been sitting on the grass near enough to hear. He always thought Uncle Rudolf was a kind man, stricter with his children than his own Papa, but the man made sure his family had warm clothes and enough to eat. Why was he saying such terrible things about the Lakota and black men? Heinrich had never seen or met a black man, but, if they were like his friends in the Lakota, they'd be good folks.

He backed away on his knees, keeping down low, so Papa would not realize he'd been eavesdropping and ran off to find Herman to tell him everything he'd just heard. He'll never believe it.

"Hey, Herman," he called.

Twelve

The revelation Papa's friend Mr. Rudolf wasn't the good man they'd thought dampened the boys' pleasure in yesterday's fun get together. Their hope and happiness evaporated the next morning. The day began murky, lit only by the thin light of dawn. Then a rap-rap-rap on the door resonated over-loud in the early morning stillness.

"Who might that be?" Papa asked, sitting up in bed. "We rarely have visitors this early except during harvest and that's still several weeks away."

"The only way to find out is to go to the door," Hilda, the ever-practical-one replied.

Emil grunted, but heaved himself up and headed down the stairs. Halfway down, he heard footsteps behind him following.

"Morning, Papa," said Heinrich.

Emil continued down and opened the door to the last person he expected to see. Wamdisapa and two of his warriors.

"Hau, my friend," he told the chief. Craning his head to spot the others in the band, Emil continued the formal greeting. "Have you eaten?"

"I have not nor can I now. I come to warn you, my friend. You must leave and go to a safe place—the white man's fort would be best. War is coming and members of my tribe and their allies will attack at nightfall. Go now and turn your team neither right nor left until you reach your destination. Others besides myself may be watching. Take as much with you as your wagon will hold, tie some of your animals behind if you can."

"Why are they going to war?"

"What the great father of the white men does not deliver, they intend to take. I do not want you and yours captured and turned into slaves for the tribe, or in any way be hurt or killed."

"You are a true friend. Thank you for warning us."

"You have proven yourself a friend worth warning many times over," the Lakota replied.

Wamdisapa half-bowed and put his hand on his chest. Emil returned the bow and gesture. The Lakotas slipped back into the obscurity of the frail light and disappeared from view.

"Come, boys. Wake your sister. We must hitch the oxen and load the wagon. *Schnell!*"

Heinrich woke Herman and Emma.

As soon as she heard the reason for haste, Mama organized the clothes and jars of canned food to take to the wagon She was Thankful Herman was still living with the family and in town snowed in. Papa and Herman led the two oxen from the barn while Heinrich pulled a crate big enough to hold half-dozen hens, which he took to the wagon. They would need eggs.

Emil turned to Herman, "Bring that short trough to the wagon. We can use it to water the cows— I'll tie them to the tailgate. The two returned to the barn. Emil retrieved two milk cows, which he tethered to the back rail of the wagon. Herman trailed him, balancing the long tin trough in both arms.

Meanwhile, Mama had Emma carrying the lighter bundles while she took the jars and cook pans. When they reached the wagon, her face split in a huge grin when she saw her husband had found the bows, which formed the framework of the hoop holding up the top of the cloth wagon cover. He and Herman toted to heavy metal arcs to the wagon and fixed them tight, tying the fabric to the bows in intervals. Between them then raised the canvas, important for a long journey in the hot summer sun. Heinrich and Herman filled a water barrel and carted it to the back of the wagon using a handcart.

While Mama was taking an inventory – matches, lamps, candles, soap, tea, coffee and blankets to use at night, Emma and Heinrich ran off to the garden to pick what might be ripe. Snapping her fingers, she exclaimed, "I forgot something."

"This will have to do, Mama," Emil said. "We're near midday already and Wamdisapa said the attack would come tonight. We must be as far as we can before darkness falls. The journey to St Cloud is at least two days--lucky for us, days are long at this time of year."

"Come on boys, Emma. Time to go. Emma, you get up on the bench of the wagon with me. Herman and Heinrich, you two ride double and stay close to the cows to keep them calm. They are no good to us if they slip their tethers and bolt."

Emil mounted the other horse they were taking with them and picked up the rein of the oxen. Better for the oxen be on lead until they were far enough away to safely respond to commands from the reins. He stood back, viewing the load, checking for balance. They were ready to go until Mama jumped off the wagon and ran back into the house. The boys looked at each other and Herman asked Emil, "Why'd she go back in?"

His answer came when she came back out carrying a silver teapot and an ornate gravy ladle. "These belonged to my mother. I couldn't bear it if anyone stole or destroyed them. After all, we brought them this far." The tone in her voice seemed to ask if it were okay.

"Good thinking, Hilda. We can't abandon our heritage," Emil said to reassure her.

He chucked at the team of oxen and took hold of their yoke. With the heavy wood crossbar in hand, he set off to the northeast for St. Cloud and safety.

Emil's urge to hurry was palpable. He understood the consequence if they failed to reach the fort in time.

Thirteen

Emil urged the oxen to maintain a smart pace. The family home for the next two days would be the road leading from the edge of Kandiyohi County where the farmhouse stood to St. Cloud, the county seat of Sterns County. The sun was broiling hot overhead when they finished loading and headed to the ford in the creek at the boundary of their farm. Sweat ran down their foreheads and soaked their shirts. The throat-parching dust from the road both helped and hurt the travelers. A dryer road prevented the sticky mud miring the wheels of the wagon—a good thing when haste was important—but the dust swirling up with each step meant a thirsty journey.

"Emma is lucky," Heinrich muttered. "She gets to ride in the wagon in the shade and away from the sun."

"Quiet, *Kleiner Knabe*, when you were her age, you were a rider, too. Shut your mouth and keep the pace," his brother said.

Emil squinted up at the sky and estimated from the position of the sun they'd have four more hours of daylight and gain some distance if the fading dusk light were bright enough to continue. "Emma, draw a bucket of water from the barrel for the team, a ladleful for your brothers, and another for me. You and your mother will need some, too, but we need to be sparing with use. We'll stop at dusk to water the animals and feed them, refill our supply. When we've tended to their needs, we can eat the sandwiches Mama made. We'll try to go a bit further. Heinrich, Herman, you two take care--your job will be to watch for holes on the road so neither ox breaks a leg."

"You want to walk at night?" Emma piped up. "What if wolves come or a great big bear?"

"Then they come, Liebchen. We'll deal with that problem if that happens. No sense worrying now. An attack by a marauding band from the local tribe is the greater risk. We must try to get as close to the fort as we can. We have weapons for wild animals, and Muttchen will be at the ready to guard us. She'll be our sentry and keep dangerous creatures at bay."

"Good thing we brought her then, isn't it?" asked Heinrich with some pride. He'd insisted the amiable mutt come along although she'd shown herself a good hunter in the past and could have survived on her own. She trotted gamely between the two boys, but she took advantage of any short stop to curl up in a nap.

"Papa, what we will do at the fort? How long will we have to stay? Will we...will we ever go back to our own house?" Emma continued, peppering her father with questions, a worried expression on her face.

"So many questions, Child, and so few answers," Emil said. "Let's keep moving and take advantage of the daylight."

As the family started down the trail, Muttchen raced to catch up. Behind them, the sky grew rosy edged in orange. A hint of cool in the breeze which picked up, but the night air arrived with unwelcome visitors. Swarms of mosquitos and black flies began their attack at dusk. The young people were glad for their long sleeves, donned to protect against the sun, now offering a barrier from the bloodsuckers, but their faces and necks remained an easy target for the persistent predatory insects.

Finally, Papa said, "Too dark now to travel with the wagon. We'll sleep here, and with the dawn rise to resume our journey."

Despite the hardness of the ground and the chiggers living in the tall dusty prairie grass, the children, exhausted, fell asleep. Emil took Hilda's hand, kissed it, and said, "We're on schedule to get there before the fighting gets serious. We owe Wamdisapa a great debt for taking the risk to warn us. Many of his fellow Lakota and Sioux would not view his action with favor. Pray God wills we reach the fort and safety and Wamdisapa and his band live through the hostilities."

Hilda reached over and patted his cheek. "Hope is eternal, my Love. Sleep now."

The shrieking of shrill bird cries announced the dawn. Emil arose and awakened the others, and Hilda started fixing breakfast. Emil sent the boys to feed and water the animals in the creek. With the two so occupied, he went through his checklist for the wagon, knots tight, wheels secure, harnesses in good condition. Emma fetched foodstuffs for her mother and saved a tidbit or two for Muttchen.

Breakfast was cold—cold oatmeal, cold tea, and yesterday's applesauce washed down with milk from a cow grateful to be relieved of overfull udders. They ate quickly. Emil hitched the oxen, and the group proceeded as on the previous day. The difference being they began this day already fatigued. Their journey continued in slow plodding, one foot in front of the other, little conversation, no laughter. They shared an intense sense of urgency. Emma's small body drooped with exhaustion, but she chose to walk and soldiered on keeping up with her brothers.

They made good time measured in oxen terms. Emil calculated if they repeated their program of the day before, they should arrive at the fort the next day, perhaps even as early as midday.

Fourteen

When the little party of weary travelers reached the outskirts of St. Cloud, their river town destination, Emil called a halt. He needed to regroup and to think because he didn't know what to expect in St. Cloud, a large city by northern Minnesota standards. He'd read abolitionist rants about slaves in the town, due in large part to the Dred Scott decision. A lady abolitionist wrote articles all the time. The opinion of the court, in this case, gave free rein to Southerner slaveholders to escape the stifling southern summers by taking a shallow draft steamboat north, bringing their human property with them. Emil had heard rumors the town's first mayor was known as a southern sympathizer, served only one term. Despite the community's reputation for Confederate leanings, a company of Union soldiers, part of the Minnesota Volunteers, occupied the town in the barracks maintained by members of the local community-.

A small squadron of blue-clad military men stopped them on the main road. "Halt, state your business," one said. Emil wasn't sure whether to answer in English, German, Swedish or French as someone in the community spoke one or more of the languages used the town and in the Union army. He'd read the founder of St. Cloud settled into three separate enclaves, one by German immigrants, one by New Englanders, and the last by Southerners, some of whom were slaveholders. When Emil explained, in German, why they'd left Paynesville, the sergeant answered in the same language and pointed toward a larger wooden stockade. Emil was glad because there'd be fewer misunderstandings.

"We're sending folks over to the Fair Haven. You might find room inside stables for your animals, too. We'll give more space when the Broker Block fortification is complete. Folks won't need to sleep on top of the counters in the general store anymore."

"*Danke*," Emil said to the burly young man. "You do a man's job these days."

Their family increased the small number of civilians already quartered in the stockade. "We're one of the first to arrive, I'm afraid," Emil murmured to Hilda. "I'm sure others will come. They must unless they build additional forts farther west. We'll be more apt to find a room. Later not so much. I suggested the young soldier ask for men to go to the Paynesville area and sound the alarm."

She looked up at him and smiled, "Oh good, Liebe, I did not feel right not warning our neighbors."

"I am in agreement. Our Lakota friends meant the warning for us—a gesture to repay our kindness. Nevertheless, we're obliged to get the word out to the others in the village—though, to my mind, in all honesty, considering the miserable way they treated the Lakota, they do not deserve such consideration."

She nodded, glancing in the direction the road guard had pointed and noted the dirt strip encased by a high log wall, which surrounded the wooden building. The debris of past men and animals littered the earth. Deep hoof prints left the dirt chopped and uneven. The air was not fresh.

Later, they learned the building once served the community as a hotel of sorts for river travelers. Never a luxury establishment, the simple compound provided a degree of safety if an attack by the Dakota took place.

Emil signed for a room after they entered the combination lunch area and lobby in the utilitarian building.

"You have the last one, Mr. Wartenburg," he said, handing Emil the key. "Your family will find it a tight fit, but we can supply one cot. The children will need to take turns sleeping on the floor."

Hilda was glad they'd thought to bring extra money along after seeing the prices on the menu. "How far are the stables? At those rates, we'll need to cook at least some of our meals by the wagon. I'm glad I packed enough for more than the two days of our trip."

"Ever the practical one," her husband answered with a faint smile.

Everyone in the family took a bundle from the wagon—clothing along with soap and sundries--and Hilda told them to bring Emil's shaving gear and gathered up valuables they did not want to leave in the wagon. When they headed up the stairs and rounded the corner to find their room, Emil and Hilda eyed each other. The innkeeper was correct. Their stay would not be altogether comfortable, but at least they'd be safe.

"You need to put everything away properly. We'll not have space to waste. Put as much as you can in the wardrobe and the rest on the shelves under the window," Hilda told the children. "If things are lying around, none of us will be comfortable."

She turned toward her husband. "I'm uneasy about all my canning I left in the wagon. If many must flee in haste, they'll arrive with nothing. This jar may help them. I realize Pastor Westerburg says we must help the poor, but charity begins at home. I think we might be able to slip a goodly portion under the bed. Then each time we go to feed the animals and collect the eggs, we can take the empty jars with us and bring back more of what 's left. Perhaps we can find a baby-bottle warmer for the kerosene lamps and warm up some of the food in the room as well as do some of our cooking near the wagon. Our excess we can share to feed other's children—our extra milk to the babies, eggs to feed us all."

"Tonight, though, we eat in the restaurant," Emil said. "Safe and sound is something to celebrate. Perhaps we'll hear news about Paynesville neighbors or meet others who had to leave."

They did not have long to wait.

Fifteen

Those trickling in later did not have the luxury of traveling with a wagon—they came on horseback, single or double, or by shank's mare, carrying hastily gathered bundles. Heinrich and Herman, wide-eyed watching the trail of refugees, pointed at one man on an improvised litter, another with a bandaged arm. The lucky ones rode on a military transport, sharing the space with wounded soldiers. The boys ran off to tell their parents what they'd about everything they'd seen.

"Loads of people came, all kinds," said Herman.

"Some were wearing bandages or others were limping," Heinrich added. "And they've a passel of kids with them."

"Did you see more women coming in than men? More women and children, I mean," Emil asked, remembering similar scenes from his past when the men of the village stayed behind to defend against the enemy.

"Ja, I guess."

"Did you recognize anyone?" Hilda asked.

"I saw one kid from my school," Herman answered.

"Then others from Paynesville must have escaped and taken refuge elsewhere. We need to go see if we can help," she said, giving Emil a meaningful glance.

Emil sought out the nearest soldier to inquire where they'd house the Paynesville refugees or the location of the camping area. The young man shrugged and said, "My guess is near the north wall. I think the area around the

Barney is full up, but they'd be able to camp in the larger open area in that direction."

"Danke," Emil said, touching his hat. "Hilda, let's collect a bucket of milk and some eggs to share with the newcomers, then head in that direction."

"Can we come, too?" the two boys asked,

"Me, too," said Emma.

"Don't expect to go empty-handed," Hilda said. "We haven't got much, but we'll try to share what we can spare."

Soon the milk and eggs were gone, soon after the young people disappeared, too.

When they neared the north wall, Herman cried, "I see Sigwulf, from school and Clara, too."

For the children, their stay at the fort had become an adventure as soon as they'd spotted friends from home. Every day seemed another church social with games and clusters of people talking—except for the columns of soldiers marching, coming and going through the gate and the number of civilians wearing bandages.

In short order, the practical Paynesville burghers organized food distribution and found space for a school. Parents decided to convert several stalls in the Broker Block stables into classrooms. A large number of students resulting from the merger of local with refugee children meant they needed three classrooms – grades one through three, four through six, and a seven eight and above. The original one-room schoolhouse became a meeting place for a de facto bureau to help newcomers find housing and for members of a family to find one another. Those who fled the violence erected a board near the former town school to post the names and home locations of their missing loved ones and ask for news of them.

The young people settled into a new normal routine. Books and slates were a problem as few thought to bring school supplies with them. A teacher from the far side of Lake Koronis took on the upper grades. Two parents acted as her assistants. Teachers sent a plea to Ft. Snelling in St. Paul to send classroom items with food in addition to the ammunition and other military supplies which made up the normal shipments sent north for the garrison.

The continuing influx prompted the garrison commander to construct further fortification on top the hill at 10th and 3rd Streets. Despite the higher location, this area the people dubbed the site Fort Holes. Newcomers noted the board listing missing family members and added the names of their own absent members along with requests for any information on them. The area nearby became a common gathering spot. The universal hope was the missing had found refuge from attacks somewhere else.

When Emil said words to that effect, Hilda arched her brows, "Ach, Emil, ever the optimist. We must look to the soldiers for news. Vain hopes save no one."

Emil's heart tugged anew as he spotted an all-together too-familiar sight. A small boy clung to a burly farmer, eyes blank, wailing like an abused animal, "Mama, Mama."

Hilda and Emil approached the man with the sad burden, "Yours?"

"*Nein*. A neighbor's," he replied. Then glancing at the boy, he mouthed, "We found him hiding under a manure wagon. Father and mother dead. His older sister not around. God help her."

Emil bent his head. This description of slaughter was so like so many he witnessed as a soldier. "Who will care for the boy?"

"We have five of our own and were lucky all escape. We'll take him in for as long as we can, but...."

"Did you know the family well?"

The stoic expression of the farmer broke, tears welling up. "The wife was a cousin of mine. We grew up in the same village in the old country. *Mein Gott—*why did we come to this god-forsaken land?"

Hilda gently patted the man's shoulder and held out a sack with a half dozen eggs. "Take these. If your wife can buy some cornmeal, she can fix you all a meal."

"Danke."

Emil and Hilda left the man standing, staring into space, holding his bag of eggs in one hand and rocking the boy in his arms. Hilda said, "I've seen the family at church, but have never spoken to them. I'm not sure why."

"I know," Emil said. "Their oldest son is the boy Heinrich fought with. The one who called the Lakota ignorant savages and accused Heinrich of being a dirty Indian lover."

Hilda's eyes widened and her hand shot over her mouth. "Oh."

Sixteen

The two walked away from the Paynesville man and his sack of eggs. Hilda reached for her husband's hand. He grasped it, and the couple walked in silence. Ignoring the conventional objections to public hand-holding their hands locked in a gesture, which seemed right at that moment. Seeing one motherless child brought back too many memories for both.

They passed a group of small children, Emma among them, playing the "Farmer in the Dell." Behind them the whoops and hollers of older children playing capture the flag or mumblety-peg. Lost in thought, the two did not notice Herman joining then, matching step for step.

"I'm old enough to help, too," he said. "The little kids are busy with school and play, but they don't understand what might have happened at home. For them, being here is a sort of a lark. I do. You've always told me in times of war, friends and family are the highest in importance. If it weren't for Wamdisapa and his people, we might not be here. I worry about Chayton, but I can't do anything to help him. Doing what I can for some of these Paynesville people is important, too—even if some of them don't deserve our assistance."

"People in need always deserve our help, Herman," Hilda said in a chiding tone.

"I knew you'd say that, but I'm coming with you, anyway. I'm way ahead of where they are in school anyway."

Emil glanced over at Hilda and put his arm around Herman's shoulder. "Let's find the sergeant and see what is really happening out there."

"Why do we need to find a sergeant, Papa?"

"Because, Son, sergeants always run the army and know what is going on."

A quick word from the sergeant sent the two toward the dock on the river. Every day Emil and his sidekick Herman made it their practice to meet the boats from farther south bringing food and other supplies. Each day they'd stop and wait until the gangplank cleared of disembarking soldiers. When the parade of blue ceased, they joined other refugee men unloading the goods for the people of the town. The job of hauling the heavy bags of flour, rice, and potatoes along with bundles of salt pork and hardtack in the hot sun was hard work. St. Cloud, being a civilian community as well as military post, created a greater need for additional foodstuffs including canned fruit and vegetables as well as ammunition and other military supplies. Many of the other men appreciated Herman's strong back and willingness to work. The hot days of August and September gave way to the cooler air of October before the tide of incoming soldiers outnumbered that of the outgoing. Larger numbers of blue-clad men wearing bloody bandages limping through the gates dulled this encouraging sign. The soldiers soon embarked for the return voyage to St. Paul. Many of the healthy men had received orders to report in at Ft. Snelling at the confluence of the Minnesota and Mississippi Rivers. Their orders read, "Prepare to move out to join other Union forces fighting the rebels of the Confederacy."

The soldier instinct in Emil fought a glimmer of disquiet at the reduced force in place to protect the families from Paynesville and surrounding area, but his rational side told him the commander would not abandon them. Still, he'd heard a rumor about guns being available with the ammunition for them included in the "unlikely event" they might need a gun to help defend the fort. "Do we need to get a gun?" Herman asked. "Heinrich and I know how to use one, but you have only one shotgun."

Seventeen

While Emil and Herman worked at the dock, Hilda and the two younger children went to the barn the community opened for the refugees where they housed their cows and chickens. In no time at all, Bessie, as the soldiers had dubbed her, was one of the refugee community's most popular residents. Her morning buckets of milk added a sense of home to their diet. None of the hens rated a name, although Emma always referred to Hannah, Mary, Magdalene, Polly, and Pookie—the three lesser hens hadn't earned a nickname and remained anonymous. Each day, Hilda reserved four eggs for their own family and gave the rest away. Eggs were fewer with the onset of cool weather and days passed with no eggs to share.

Hilda grew impatient with those acting as though they were entitled. No surprise that they were the ones who did the least for the small colony of exiles. When she shared her exasperation with Emil, he shrugged and said, "No different from ordinary days. They're the same ones who bring the least to the church suppers."

"Doesn't make it right," she retorted.

"No, but we deal with what we can solve."

A young soldier overheard their conversation. "You're both right," he said. His one arm in a sling, he tipped his head toward the gate. "They tell me things are winding down. Most of the active fighting seems done and over. With luck, you'll be out of here and back home soon."

"This is great news. Do you know any more? "

"What they've told me is some units are hot on the trail of some of the Sioux ringleaders. They'll probably hang the bastards."

"And the Lakota?" Herman interjected. "What have you heard about them?"

"Is Lakota a name they call themselves? I don't abide by any of that nonsense. An Indian is an Indian in my book. We need to string them all up — mop up this operation and get back to fighting Johnny Reb," the soldier replied, his tone showing his low opinion of Native Americans.

He didn't notice the shocked expression on the face of the two youngsters who'd come up from behind him. Heinrich bent over to pick up a rock, and Emma seemed about to follow his example. Their father's harsh tone stopped them in mid-pitch. "*My* children do not act this way. Both of you may pick a switch on the way back to our billet."

He then turned toward the man in blue. "And you, young man, need to grow up. Such talk doesn't even belong in a playground game, nor in real life. War brings out the worst in all men, but real men rise above such hatefulness."

"How would you know, old man?" the soldier sneered.

Emil whirled. "I spent years in the military and learned this in the service of two brave commanders. When our prince ordered us to raze villages with women and children for no reason other than their beliefs, moral men moved slow enough to allow as many as possible to escape.

"Try that in our army, and you'd end up shot," was the reply.

"Better to disobey and ascend to heaven than obey and face judgment by all that is holy as a sinner," Emil said. "Come, children."

"Papa, that man was mean," Emma said.

He nodded.

"But, Papa, was he right? Do we need to leave here? Why? I like living in St. Cloud. I've got more kids to play with and more toys. Frau Muller is a nicer teacher than Miss Koepp. Can't we stay and go to school here? Please. Please, can we?"

"Emma, begging does not become you. What have I told all of you about speaking ill of your elders?" he chided, his grim face masking an inner fury.

"Not to do it," she answered, hanging her head.

"Back to our billet," Emil said. His tone signaling the conversation was over. Heinrich and Emma lagged well back, sharing their unhappiness at the prospect of leaving newfound friends. Preoccupied with fear and worry over the fate of Wamdisapa and the others in "their" band of Lakota, Emil didn't notice.

His unease was evident, and his worry soon proved correct.

Eighteen

News began to filter on the uprising. According to the reports, the bloodiest encounters occurred far south of Paynesville. Emil shared tea one morning with the fort commander familiar with the history of government Lakota relations. He explained how Thomas J. Galbraith, as Indian Agent, enforced the federal assimilation policies and withheld food and other supplies to force the Dakota into conforming with white ideals.

"I don't know the whole story about his antics," the commander said, "but the rumors of government corruption in the Indian Affairs Department have been rampant. All the corruption angered and frustrated the Dakotas. I heard in early 1862, Abraham Lincoln appointed George E. H. Day as the special agent to investigate inappropriate activities. Day uncovered what he called "voluminous and outrageous frauds upon the Indians." He reported his finding to William Dole, Commissioner of Indian Affairs who chose to ignore him, in fact, called his fear imaginary. My source tells me Day was so frustrated, he traveled to Washington and claimed in a letter numerous violations existed within Indian affairs in Minnesota. According to Day, if the double-dealing continued, violence would result. Few took him at his word, but no person stationed in this part of the country expressed surprised when a hundred or more members of the Dakota Soldiers' Lodge Sioux bands opted to attack and take the stores of food they felt were theirs."

"Looking through their eyes, this was a justifiable attack," Emil commented.

"Not a chance. Those savages got more than they deserved. Anyway, in late August, they attacked New Ulm and set fire to the town. Two days later the townsfolk evacuated and fled to safety in the nearest fort in Mankato. Col. Henry Sibley, who headed our forces up this way, sent soldiers to subdue the uprising and met the Crow and the Dakota for the final battle at Wood Lake. The government sent over seven thousand soldiers to defeat the tribes. Forced to leave their camps and abandon supplies, many Indian women and children starved or froze when winter set in. Their men abandoned them. Shiftless lot, all of them."

"War makes men make for bad decisions. The results most often are hardest on the innocent," Emil said. "I've seen similar things all too often in the old country."

"Anyway, our forces captured several hundred warriors and hung almost forty. I heard some got the noose even though they found little evidence against them. That's what they get when they go to war against the United States," the commander said.

When Emil returned to the family quarter and shared this news, the family's worry over the fate of their Lakota friends deepened. What if they'd hung one of the local band? Soldiers said the judge ordered all seven Dakota tribes of southwestern Minnesota into exile and sent them three to a desolate area of the Dakota Territory. Would Wamdisapa and his family still be living near our farm? Would they ever learn what happened to them?

With the tide turning against the uprising, the family felt safe in returning to the farm. They packed the wagon and then joined others for their final meal in St. Cloud. For the children, saying goodbye to the new friends they'd met during their stay was hard—their parents, too. Heinrich and Emma's long faces showed their sadness. They all shared names and addresses and promised to try to stay in touch. Emil and Hilda understood the reluctance of the children had at leaving, but their worry over the condition of the farmhouse and outbuildings outweighed any hesitation.

Their return trip in December to the Paynesville area seemed to take twice as long as their flight to St. Cloud. A fierce north wind blew with a sharp edge making for cold days. At days end, they had little to look forward to except some slight relief by sleeping on the lee side of the wagon. The autumn sun set hours sooner than in summer, bringing on a dark cloud-covered night sky broken by some star-filled night open spaces. The family had no option but to build a fire each night to keep warm, and, on some days, they wore almost all the clothes they'd brought in the wagon.

Herman noticed his father was glancing skyward often. "What are you looking for, Papa?" he asked.

"I'm scanning for the patches of dark gray signaling a bad storm. If the weather turns bad, we will need to stop and dig a deep hole to give us more shelter. Should the temperature drop too much while we are out in the open, we are in danger of freezing."

Herman's head snapped towards Emil as Heinrich caught up alongside. "Who's freezing?" he asked.

"No one yet—which is why both of you need to pick up every branch and cow patty you see should we have a need for additional fuel."

The two boys eyed each other grimacing. "Lakota killing settlers, the weather killing settlers, wolves eating travelers next?" Heinrich said under his breath.

"Not if we work together," Herman answered, playing the part of an older, wiser brother.

Mama hopped off the wagon, "Emil, why don't you ride for a while. I can walk. You're no good to us if you get too tired."

Emil tried to protest, but, in the end, he capitulated. "Emma, you get in back, your brothers and I will take turns driving the oxen."

Two days later, they still had not spotted any signs of life. No dairy cows in the pasture, no geese charging to challenge them. The dead crops stood unharvested, which was no surprise, but some far off acreages seemed more charred than dead.

"Do you suppose they had a grass fire here, Emil?" Hilda asked.

His eyes zigged back and forth before he answered, "Yes, but my guess the cause was not lightning, but fire from another means."

Hilda's hand shot to her mouth in alarm. "Do you mean…?"

"I do, Liebchen, signs of battle. Do you remember the Schmidts? The ones who lived west of this road leading to our farm?"

"Yes."

"The smoke from their chimney should be over there…I see nothing coming out of the stack. That's not good."

"Neither do I — no, not good at all," she answered. "But at least the children aren't talking about seeing their old friends again or asking us why some friend's house isn't there."

Worry showed on both faces, a worry that deepened the closer they got to their farm. The mood was no less grim in the clump of children lagging behind. Heinrich was first to notice the missing trail of smoke. As soon as he shared his observation, even

Emma realized what might have happened. The two boys whispered to each other, not wanting to worry their parents. "Old people don't see much," Heinrich murmured.

In a couple of hours, neither young nor old folks could make any excuses. The farmhouse, which should have been within a hundred yards away, was gone. Only a blackened foundation remained. A jumbled cluster of boards missing the tall hay, normally nearby, comprised what remained of the barn. A brighter note was one remaining side of the grove, which circled the house on the windy side. They would have shelter tonight. Dusk was already deepening, and their farm would need to wait until tomorrow.

"We'll pull the wagon in here," Emil ordered. "We can take advantage of the trees blocking the wind. The clouds cut off the remaining light, and the road won't be safe for the oxen."

"Papa, this is creepy. There might be ghosts here," Emma said.

"Fire drives away spirits, Liebchen. No worries for you here," he answered trying for a reassuring smile.

"Heinrich, Herman, you feed the animals. I'll pull the wagon in and start a fire for Mama to fix us some supper. I'll take a torch and see if I find anything."

His voice trailed off, as he did not want to voice his innermost fears. Neighbors might have perished along with the house and barn. *How many more? How many more have died in this senseless war caused by a faithless government?* He shook his head as he led the oxen to the edge of the grove.

After their quick meal, Emil put a branch into the fire to make a torch. "I'll go with you, Papa," Herman said.

73

Emil hesitated, but Herman needed to grow up and face adult problems someday. He nodded. The two set off in the direction of the foundation.

"Nothing here, Papa," Herman reported from his side of the stone circle which had supported a house.

"Nor here," Emil replied. "Barn, next."

The two boys poked through the debris of a barn and found nothing of the family who had lived there. No animals, no tools, no seed or feed. They discovered the cause of the fire, a half-burned arrow left stuck on one board.

Emil bent and found a grimmer object. Flies buzzed around the upper portion. He stood and shooed his sons toward the wagon.

The boys' eyes met. *What was he keeping from them? Or who?*

Nineteen

The hours passed and, although the family could see their grove from the top of the hill, the trees obscured any sight of the farmhouse.

Herman, who now considered himself part of the adult contingent, muttered to his father, "Will our house still be there?"

"'Depends on who came by, Son," he answered. "We can only trust that the friendship we had with Wamdisapa's band proved a true one. The pastor teaches us 'Do unto others, as ye would have others do unto you." We did not wrong them and should not expect them to wrong us—but if another band came....'"

Hilda spoke up from behind the two. "Your papa should know. When he was in the Imperial service, he lived through many battles and saw countless villages destroyed. The houses with residents who'd shown kindness to others often survived."

"Often, but not always," Emil cautioned. He flicked the reins on the back of the team, urging them forward. When they rounded the corner, a whoop went up. Their house was still there, and the barn and haystack were intact. Hilda threw her arms around Emil, tears running down her cheeks. She opened the embrace, extending one arm. The children crowded in in a group hug. Even the air smelled better as they soaked up the love and relief they were experiencing.

"Let's go in, Emil," Hilda said, her voice shaking. "We need to see what is inside."

Emil cleared his throat, "Herman, Heinrich, you two go to the barn and check on how much feed might be there. Emma, you go to the hen house. If any laying hens are still around, you might find eggs."

"Yes, Papa," they chorused.

"He's trying to get rid of us again," Herman muttered to Heinrich as soon as they were out of earshot of their parents.

After the children ran to their tasks, Emil turned toward his wife, took her hand, and said, "Come, Liebchen. Let's go home."

The two crossed the porch into the kitchen. Their heads swiveled as they viewed what was there. The pans were on the wall, the dishes in the Yankee pantry. Hilda bent over, holding her face in her hands. She tucked herself under Emil's shoulder and reached around him. "A miracle, Emil, a miracle from God," she said.

The screen door slamming shattered the silence.

"Papa, the pigs are still in the sty, and we saw some of the dairy cows we left behind, too."

"How can that be?" Emil asked. "Who fed them, milked them? I doubt God himself came down to care for our animals."

"Maybe a neighbor," Hilda suggested.

Herman shook his head, "I don't think so. We're all alone out here now. Ours was the first house we came to with no damage. Where would they be living?"

"And why wouldn't they be tending their own animals?" added Heinrich.

From the other side of the kitchen, Mama's voice, "Wait—all I see amiss is one stove lid is broken. See, the big one over the soup pot."

Her answer was all around confusion. No one put forth a guess.

"Looks like we spoke too soon," Emil said trying to hide an amused smile.

She sniffed. "In that case, I guess I need to fix supper so we all can sleep in our own beds tonight … if …if…"

Three sets of feet pounded up the stairs. "The beds, they're here, Mama, they're here."

"And Kleine Katze was asleep on my bed," exclaimed Emma.

Mama did not look pleased, but conceded with a sigh, "Ach, I guess she earned the privilege. She kept the mice out of the larder."

"Ja, maybe, but she left the heads in there, on my pillow."

Emil smiled at his family. "We are together and alive. More fortunate than many."

"Come, Kinder. Let us bow our heads and give thanks to the almighty who has intervened on our behalf," Emil said.

The family made a small circle and stood in silence with their heads down until Emil lifted his head and said, "Tonight we sleep and rest from our journey. On the morrow, the boys and I will leave to learn the fate of our neighbors and the citizens of Paynesville. Let us hope others shared our good fortune."

The three set out the next morning with rigid shoulders and long faces. Emil hoped for the best but expected the worst. At first, the worse of his fears seemed realized. Farm after farm between their house and the town of Paynesville held only charred buildings. Finally, on the ride down one driveway, they encountered people.

"*Guten Tag*," Emil cried as they approached.

"*God Eftermiddag*," the tall blond man standing by a lone wagon answered.

"They're Swedes," Herman whispered to his brother.

"We are just back from the fort at St. Cloud. The whole county seemed to be empty. Was there a great loss of life?"

"Great enough. I'm told over twenty perished, and y more would have had there not been a great exodus away from the conflict. The wagons filled the roads in a constant stream leaving much of the land vacant and possessions for the taking by the marauding bands of Indians. Most of our dead were from nearby communities. I learned this when several of us who were still in the area heard of a meeting in Paynesville and took care to attend."

"A meeting? Why ever for?"

"The townspeople wrote the governor and requested soldiers be sent to protect the settlers and have them build fortifications to protect life and limb from further attack."

"Did the Governor send help?"

"Indeed, they dispatched soldiers who helped construct fortifications."

'This explains why not so many were with us in St. Cloud. They found refuge closer by."

"Ja, that is so," the big Swede said. "By the way, my name is Arne Almquist."

"Emil Wartenburg... and these are my sons Herman and Heinrich."

The two shook hands and bobbed their heads in the polite if belated greeting.

"Are others returned as well?"

"Not so many yet. Not much left to return to and folks are cautious. I suspect some will never return if the soldiers are not posted here for the duration."

"In that case, my boys and I are happy to lend you a hand in rebuilding your home."

"Heinrich started to ask a question but decided he ought not. He asked himself instead. *What about Chayton and the others in Wamdisapa's band of Lakota?*

Twenty

As the days passed, after two weeks life on the farm soon seemed almost normal to the young folks. They remembered friends they'd made in St. Cloud and penned a letter, but routine eased their separation. Each child had the same chores they had before the emergency flight to the fort at St Cloud. Hilda resumed her normal activities in the kitchen. Emil divided his time between farm work and making a circuit of the burned-out properties to see if any more had returned and need temporary lodging. The winter screamed in with a vengeance forcing a family decision to send the children into town until spring to attend the makeshift school that sprung up. Conditions on the road were too hazardous for daily travel, but education for their children was a priority for Emil and Hilda.

"Mama and I will hold down the fort until you are back. The cows won't drop any calves until spring, nor will the sows produce piglets. We can do whatever we need to do keep this running. When there is a break in the weather, I will take the sleigh to buy provisions, see you while I'm there, and chat with the townsfolk for the latest news."

"And I will come as well," Mama added. "I will need to buy fabric and thread to make clothes because you all will grow out of what you have now. I doubt any of the peddlers will come this far with the blizzards coming as close together as they've been."

Emma started to cry, scared to be alone and away from home, but Herman and Heinrich were able to reassure her. "You won't be with strangers. You know Arthur and Ruth."

Emil and Hilda had arranged for the children to stay in the home of Hilda's cousin Arthur. His wife and he had returned from a safe location at a closer fortification and had agreed to take in the three. To do their part and not impose on their hosts, Mama pulled jar after jar out of the larder and baked several loaves of bread for them to take with them "for their keep."

Emil and Hilda stayed overnight with Arthur and Ruth until well into the next day. Keen to learn more of the events, which took place after their flight to St. Cloud. Bit by bit, the story came out. Ruth explained the morning started out as usual with townspeople shopping and working their gardens then refugees started filtering in with stories of brutal attacks by roving bands of Dakota and Chippewa. The men quickly constructed a sod fort to give more security until materials to construct one of wood became available. Many of the residents still did not feel secure and left to existing forts manned by soldiers of the Minnesota Volunteers. Emil stopped in the mayor's office for a more official report. The mayor was talkative.

"Our town remained near empty for a while," Mayor Nehring explained. "Once the refugees showed up with the stories of Indian attacks, a good many wanted a more secure place. 'Course we built some sod barriers, but some folks are never seem satisfied. They took off for Fair Haven once a few soldiers were free to escort them. To be fair, a bunch of houses burned which made them even more disinclined to stay.""

"We headed out the other way, to the fort at St. Cloud. This explains why we didn't see many from around here. I was concerned how many were killed."

"Naw, we go lucky that way, and one of the local bands showed up and helped us. We sent out search parties to pick up those families "Those what were burned out."

"Really, to help? What band was that?" Emil asked.

"Ach, I don't know one Indian from another. The commander from Fair Haven says the Governor gave amnesty to bands who helped the settlers so they don't have to move to that god-forsaken stretch in the Dakota Territory."

"We had a band living by us, good neighbors. Helped us. Wamdisapa's band of Lakota," Emil said.

"Huh, ain't heard of them, but I'll pass that on."

"Thanks, Mayor."

When Emil returned to his cousins, he shared with Hilda the news "Helpful Indians" got special treatment." Her eyes met his. "Let's hope they considered our friends 'helpful.'"

The two left the next morning and Emil did not tell the boys his plan was to ride over to where the Wamdisapa's village was located to check on the well-being of his band of Lakota. The rumors were the governor ordered all the local Indians exiled, even those considered helpful, driven out of their homes.

Yet another blizzard delayed his ride out to the Lakota village. Emil did not want to leave Hilda alone and responsible for tending the animals in such a severe storm, but, as soon as the sun reappeared, he saddled up.

Coming over the rise, which signaled the village was nearby, Emil's hopes dropped. No smoke, no activity, no horses hobbled outside the dwellings. His eyes grew moist as he entered the empty settlement. Tears were unmanly, yet he felt a trickle down his cheek. He nurtured the small kernel of hope he had left.

I refuse to mourn our friends unless I have firm knowledge.

He banged on the pommel of the saddle in futility, dreading having to tell his family what he'd learned.

Epilogue

Three weeks later, the children were back home for a school break. As the five sat at the breakfast table over eggs and biscuits, a knock sounded at the door and they heard deep voices muttering in the background.

Emil and Hilda hesitated, but Emil arose and went to the door. Outside stood Wamdisapa and a young man he didn't recognize.

To mask his surprise, Emil asked, "Have you eaten, my friend?"

The Lakota put his hand to his cheek, "Hau. We come not for food today, but for shame. One of my band has dishonored all Lakota."

"I don't understand," Emil said.

"Speak," Wamdisapa ordered his companion. "He comes to apologize for wronging our friends. He broke the cover on your iron cook place with his tomahawk. The Lakota does not destroy the possessions of those they call friend."

"I beg forgiveness, sir. I did not know whose house this was. I am less than the excrement of a weasel. I beg your forgiveness and pledge to make amends."

"We saw the chimney smoke and rejoiced to see life here once more. All in our band knew yours was the only settler's house left standing. Those who mistreated us paid a price. A friend should not," the chief said sternly.

"We forgive you," Emil said. He looked over at his family and said in as solemn tones, "Because we offered our friendship, the Lakota gave us theirs. Remember this as you grow up. Friendship is the glue holding humankind together."

"Now, have you eaten, my friend?" he asked, as Hilda brought out more biscuits.

His father and Wamdisapa were talking when Herman spotted movement at the edge of the grove and recognized the person who stepped out of the shadows of the trees.

With a whoop, he ran out to meet the person. Halting, he pulled himself up tall and said to Chayton, "Have you eaten, my friend?"

The two stood a shorter, smaller duplicate of their fathers.

The author graduated from college in Minnesota then spent time as a direct mail copywriter in Missouri and in New York as a communication officer, assistant editor, and freelancer, until another move put 0writing into hiatus. A few years ago, she hit the keyboard again and has had 3 novels and various short stories published.

Writing as Estee Kessler, she has had three tongue-in-cheek paranormal novels published. Both featured a most unlikely detective team. The series includes My Partner Jakup the Jay, J&R Rides Again, and Jaybird in a Lei. Several other manuscripts are in progress.

Haw Kola, Lakota Fall, a story set in 1862 deals with hot button topics facing us in the twentieth century. A fictional account based on an historical incident in Minnesota, the book touches on racial prejudice, minority profiling, bullying, victimization, and unlikely friendship. A morality tale for Middle and High School age, Haw Kola illustrates difficult concepts in an age appropriate fashion.

1. Who was most responsible for the uprising – the settlers? The Native Americans? The Government? Why—your answer.

2. Why didn't the immigrant settlers speak English? What language did they use in public? At home? Did all settlers speak the same language?

3. Why did the immigrants come to Minnesota?

4. Was Heinrich right in having a fight with Adolf…or should he have ignored what Adolf said about his Lakota friends? What would you have done?

5. Would you like to have lived on a farm in 1860? In Minnesota?

6. Would you have been glad or sad when the stable school opened in St. Cloud?

7. Do all your friends look like you? Why or why not?

8. What have you learned from the story?

www.ingramcontent.com/pod-product-compliance
Lightning Source LLC
Chambersburg PA
CBHW020547130626
46552CB00007B/2797